THOMAS
and the Rumors

AND OTHER THOMAS THE TANK ENGINE STORIES

Random House 🏠 New York
A Random House PICTUREBACK® Book
Photographs by David Mitton, Terry Palone, and Terry Permane for
Britt Allcroft's production of *Thomas the Tank Engine and Friends*.

Thomas the Tank Engine & Friends

A BRITT ALLCROFT COMPANY PRODUCTION
Based on The Railway Series by The Rev W Awdry
Copyright © Gullane (Thomas) LLC 2002.
Photographs © Gullane (Thomas) Limited 2002.
All rights reserved under International and Pan-American Copyright Conventions.
Published in the United States by Random House, Inc., New York, and simultaneously
in Canada by Random House of Canada Limited, Toronto.
www.randomhouse.com/kids   www.thomasthetankengine.com
Library of Congress Cataloging-in-Publication Data
Thomas and the rumors and other Thomas the tank engine stories.
p. cm. — (A Random House pictureback book)
"Based on The railway series by the Rev. W. Awdry." — T.p. verso.
CONTENTS: Thomas and the rumors — James and the trouble with trees — Happy ever after.
ISBN 0-375-81372-1
1. Children's stories, English. [1. Railroads—Trains—Fiction.]
I. Awdry, W. Railway series. II. Random House pictureback. PZ7 .T3694596 2002 [E]—dc21 2001019850
Printed in the United States of America   February 2002 10 9 8 7 6 5 4 3 2 1
PICTUREBACK, RANDOM HOUSE and colophon, and PLEASE READ TO ME and colophon are registered trademarks of Random House, Inc.

THOMAS AND THE RUMORS

Thomas the Tank Engine loves his branch line. One day, when he stopped at a small station, some children looked sad.

"They've closed our playground and our favorite sand pit."

"Teacher says the sand is soiled and too dirty to play in."

"Please help us, Thomas."

"I'll see what I can do," replied Thomas kindly.

Thomas hoped things weren't quite as bad as the children had made them out to be but, as he passed their playground, a large sign read, "Playground closed until further notice."

"The children were right," thought Thomas sadly.

He puffed into the yards and was just about to tell the other engines about the playground when Percy rushed in.

"You look glum, little Percy," said Gordon.

"Sir Topham Hatt told Driver that he's using Harold to show a visitor the island instead of using any of us engines!"

"Despicable!" said Gordon.

"Disgusting!" snorted Henry.

"Engines are meant to take visitors around our island. Not that whirlybird thing!" James exclaimed.

Gordon was the first to see Harold. "Harold thinks he can go faster than me. I'll show him!"

Next it was Henry's turn. "Sir Topham Hatt has chosen Harold because he thinks he's more important than me. Well, he's not! Harold can't fly through tunnels!"

Percy stopped by a signal on his branch line near a field where sheep were grazing. Harold hovered for a while, then buzzed away. "I know what he's doing! He's counting sheep!" And Percy puffed along his line feeling much better about things.

That evening, the engines talked about the situation. "Harold wants to get rid of us," said Gordon.

"He doesn't need tunnels," added Henry.

"Don't worry, he's just counting sheep," said Percy.

"Counting sheep . . . pah!" snorted Gordon. "He's counting how many engines he can get rid of. He'll see how useful I am tomorrow."

Thomas wanted to mention the children's playground, but solving the mystery of Harold and the visitor came first.

The next day, Gordon was traveling to collect his train. "We'll show that whirlybird just how fast you can go, Gordon," said his driver. But because they were watching Harold, they missed a signal and went onto the wrong line.

Gordon was traveling to trouble—ahead was a tunnel under repair. His driver reduced steam and braked hard, but it was too late.

Later, Thomas pulled Gordon clear with the breakdown train. Sir Topham Hatt spoke severely to Gordon's driver.

"Will Gordon be scrapped, sir?" asked Thomas sadly.

"What makes you think that?" said Sir Topham Hatt.

Thomas decided to pluck up courage. "Because the engines think the visitor is here to see if we can be replaced by Harold."

Sir Topham Hatt laughed. "Well, the engines are wrong, and you shouldn't listen to rumors, Thomas. This gentleman is making a playground for the children. It was easier to find a suitable site from up in the air."

"And what's more," said the visitor, "that tunnel sand will be perfect for the playground. Sand we found by accident, you might say."

Sir Topham Hatt still uses Harold to fly above the island, but all the engines know that Harold isn't spying on them; he is just being very useful.

JAMES AND THE TROUBLE WITH TREES

Thomas the Tank Engine had been working in the coal yards all day. The little blue engine was covered in coal dust. "We can't clean you up tonight, Thomas," said his driver. "There's a problem with the hosepipe."

"Bother," said Thomas. "A bath would make me feel much better. The others are sure to say I look silly."

But the engines were too busy arguing to notice Thomas.

James was talking loudest of all. "I deserve a new coat of paint. Sir Topham Hatt says I'm the pride of the line and—"

"Rubbish," huffed Henry. "We're all the pride of the line."

"It's been like this all day," confided Percy to Thomas. "James is getting a new coat of paint and won't stop boasting about it."

"Why James? I'm the one who needs a new coat—look at me!"

"I'd rather not," retorted James. "You're not a pleasant sight, and wouldn't understand the needs of a really important engine!"

Thomas was fuming.

Next morning, as James was being repainted, Henry had an accident. "If you can't push cars properly, Henry, why not talk to a tree instead—you know how much you like the forest!"

"As a matter of fact, Bossy Boiler, Sir Topham Hatt is inspecting the island for trees that are too close to the line. He's worried they might cause trouble."

"Pah," laughed James. "If I came upon a tree, I'd just push it aside."

"Really!" Henry replied.

Soon James was showing off his paintwork. "Make way for an important engine."

"You wouldn't feel important if one of those trees crashed on you—you'd feel hurt," reproached Percy.

"Rubbish! It wouldn't dare!"

"You should be careful, James—trees can be just as powerful as engines," advised Terence.

"Oh, please!" snorted James. "Now excuse me. Sir Topham Hatt needs me to pull the Express!" And he huffed away.

But James was wrong. "You must go to the yards and collect an important goods train, James. It's heavy, so be careful," said Sir Topham Hatt.

"But, sir, I've just been repainted. Can't Thomas or Percy do it? They're dirty and like working with freight cars."

"Really Useful Engines don't argue."

So James didn't.

By the time he arrived at the yards, the weather had changed for the worse. "Your color's nice, James—pity about your face, though," said a freight car.

James ignored them and set off. Soon they came to a hill, and his driver knew they were in for a difficult time. An old tree close to the track was being blown by the strong winds, and the rain had weakened the slope.

All of a sudden, the tree moved. "Ooh, help!" cried James. "Go away!" But, of course, the tree couldn't. James tried to reverse away from the tree, but his train was too heavy.

Then he heard a whistle. "It's Thomas!" called his driver. James felt embarrassed and worried that Thomas would laugh at him. But Thomas didn't. He knew this was no time for teasing.

"*Peep, peep* . . . I'm ready," whistled Thomas.

"So am I," replied James. "As ready as I'll ever be."

They were just in time!

Later, James spoke to Thomas. "Percy and Terence were right to warn me. Thank you for rescuing me, Thomas."

"Oh, that's all right. We engines must pull together, whatever the weather!"

Just then Edward bustled in. "Sir Topham Hatt thinks you're both brave engines. Thomas—you're going to have a new coat of paint. And, James—Sir Topham Hatt says that tomorrow you'll pull the special Express."

Everyone was very happy.

HAPPY EVER AFTER

The engines on the Island of Sodor love holiday time.

Percy was taking some freight cars to the docks. Terence the Tractor was working in a field close to the line. "Hello, Percy. Nice day for it, isn't it?"

Percy was confused. "Nice day for what?"

"Mrs. Kyndley's daughter is getting married today."

"Oh yes, of course."

But when Percy saw Mrs. Kyndley, she was standing by her gate waving a red flag.

"What's the matter?" asked the driver.

"I've forgotten about the 'good luck' package for the bride!"

"What's a 'good luck' package?"

"It must contain something old, something new, something borrowed, and something blue. Can you help, please?"

Percy didn't know how, but his driver was determined. "We'll certainly try."

Percy had to stop at Edward's station to take on water. "We've got to find a 'good luck' package. Do you know what that is?"

"Oh yes, indeed. Something old, something new—"

"—something borrowed, and something blue," Percy cut in. "But where do we find them?"

Edward smiled. "They're probably staring you in your smokebox. Now I have to fetch my special train. I'm taking guests to the wedding."

When Percy arrived at the docks, he looked all around him. Suddenly he saw a freight car. It was loaded with a new set of shiny buffers. "Look, look! The 'something new'!"

"You're quite right, Percy," said his driver. "Those buffers are just the ticket. I'll speak to the foreman."

He returned shortly. "Foreman said we can use them and borrow the freight car as well, so that's two things we've found. Something borrowed and something new!"

"But what about the other things?"

"I'm sure we'll find them, too. Now we'd best be on our way."

As Percy was shunting more freight cars into a siding, he heard a voice. "Hello, Percy." There was old Slow Coach, who he and Thomas had rescued from scrap.

"You're it!" squeaked Percy.

"I'm what 'it'?" said the coach.

"The 'something old' for the wedding!" And Percy explained. "Now we only have to find something blue, but what—and where?"

"You'll see," said his driver.

At last they reached the village where the wedding was to take place. Ahead was an old engine shed. "What do you think of this, Percy?" laughed his driver.

"Well, bust my boiler . . . Thomas! What are you doing here?"

"I'm the 'something blue,'" replied Thomas.

"Now, Percy," said his driver, "Mrs. Kyndley's chosen you to be her special guest."

When the bride and groom left the church for the party, Sir Topham Hatt addressed everybody. "Ladies and gentlemen, may I present the 'good luck' package—something old, something new, something borrowed, something blue! All found by Percy and his crew!" The engines whistled and everyone cheered.

"Thank you, Thomas, and thank you, Percy," said the bride. "It's the best 'good luck' package ever!" And she kissed Percy. Thomas laughed as Percy blushed bright red.

"I love weddings," sighed
Percy that night.
"Did you enjoy your kiss?"
asked Thomas.

But Percy was embarrassed
and pretended to be asleep.